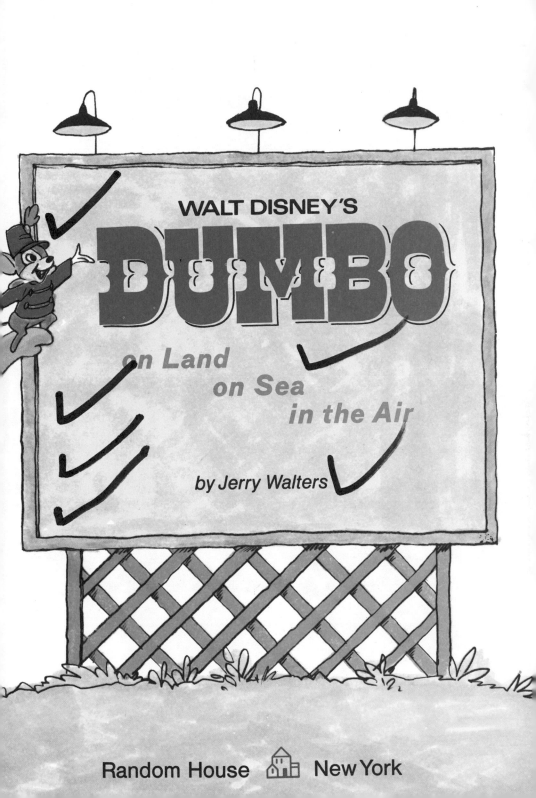

WALT DISNEY'S

DUMBO

on Land
on Sea
in the Air

by Jerry Walters

Random House 🏠 New York

Library of Congress Cataloging in Publication Data

Walters, Jerry.

Dumbo on land, on sea, in the air.

When the train breaks down on the way to their
opening performance, Dumbo and the other circus
animals must find other means of transportation.

[1. Circus stories] I. Title. PZ10.3.W203Du [E] 72-7397
ISBN 0-394-82518-7 ISBN 0-394-92518-1 (lib. bdg.)

Manufactured in the United States of America

R S T U V   2 3 4 5 6 7 8 9

Mrs. Jumbo put her big, yellow case onto the train.
"That is that!" she said. "Now the circus is ready to go."

All the animals were in their seats.
But the train did not start.
They waited and waited and waited.
The train still did not move.

Finally Mrs. Jumbo
looked out the window.

"Dumbo," she said to her son.
"Go see why the train does not start.
We will be late."

Dumbo went to the front of the train.
There he saw Casey, Jr., the engine.
Poor Casey! He had lost two wheels.
And he seemed to be falling apart.

Dumbo told his mother the bad news.
"Oh, dear," she said. "What will we do?
The circus opens in Boston in just four days."

"I will find a way for us to get there," said Dumbo.
He flapped his long, floppy ears. He flew into the air.
Dumbo was the only flying elephant in the world.
His friend Timothy, the mouse, sat on Dumbo's nose.

Together, Dumbo and Timothy
flew over the city.

"Look!" called Timothy. "A ship.
We can go to Boston on a ship.
It must be fun to travel on the water."

Dumbo landed on the deck
of the great big ship.

"Can you take our circus
to Boston?" he asked
the ship's captain.

"I will be glad to take you,"
said the captain.

Mrs. Jumbo was very happy when she heard the news.

"Follow me," she called to the other animals.

"I will lead you to the ship."

Each animal had his own way
of getting onto the ship.

Mrs. Jumbo walked across a little bridge.
She was so fat that it almost broke in two.

The giraffe grabbed the rail with his long legs.
The bear swung over on a big hook.
The rhino tried to climb through the life-saver.

Look out, everybody! Here comes Tiger Jim on a rope!
If he isn't careful, a flying fox will hit him.

"Glad to see you!" said the captain.
"Please feel right at home here."

The monkeys felt right at home.
They started swinging from the lights.

Mrs. Jumbo went to her room.

"Oh, my," she said. "That bed
looks a little small for me.
I had better see if it fits."
And up the ladder she went.

Crash! Mrs. Jumbo landed on the floor.
The bed was certainly too small.

Harry Hippo wanted to go upstairs.
The stairs were tiny. He was big.
His friends had to push and push
. . . and push.

Wham! They pushed a little too hard.
Harry crashed through the door
and banged into the poor captain.
The captain fell through the steering wheel
and hit the table.

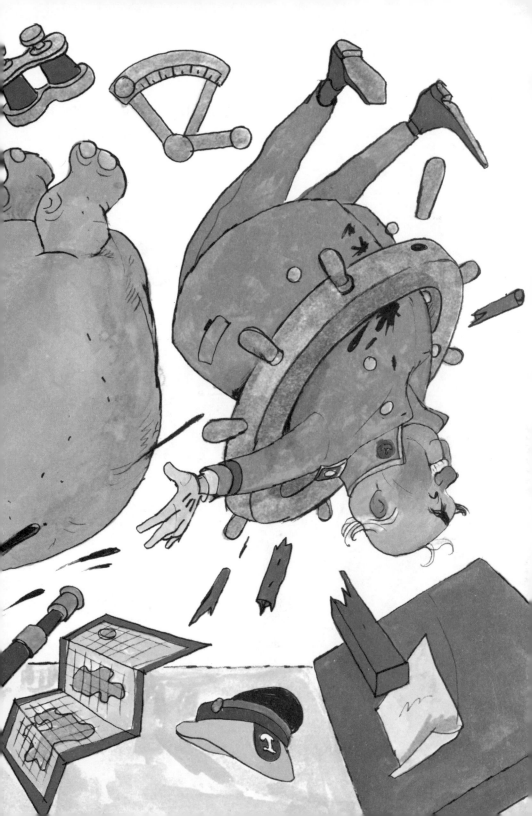

The captain was very, very angry.
"Pack your bags!" he shouted.

"I will not take this circus
any farther. Get off my ship!"

Dumbo and Timothy flew away
from the ship as fast as they could.
Now they had to find another way
to get to Boston.

They did not have much time.
The circus had to be there
in just three days.

Soon they came to an airport.

"Look at that big helicopter," shouted Timothy. "Maybe we can use that. Then *everybody* can fly— just like you and me."

The helicopter man was glad
to follow Dumbo and Timothy
to the ship.

When the animals saw
the helicopter coming,
they all began to cheer.
"Hurray for Dumbo!"
they shouted.

Dumbo's friends began to climb
aboard the helicopter. What fun!
The monkeys ran up the giraffe's neck,
while a big net carried Mrs. Jumbo.
The fox had a nice ride on her trunk.

At last the animals were all set.

Everybody had his own place.

The seal even had water to splash in.

What a good way to travel!

As they rode, they looked out the windows
at the bright blue sky.
They had never gone so fast before.
Flying was certainly fun. . . . But suddenly——

The wind began to blow. The sky grew black.
Lightning flashed and the rain poured down.
The helicopter began to shake.
All of the animals were afraid.

"Dumbo, you must get us out of here!"
shouted Mrs. Jumbo.

Dumbo and Timothy flew down
toward the ground.
It was hard to see in the rain.
But they found a big parking place.
There were trucks and cars on it.
There was also room for a helicopter.

The helicopter landed,
and the animals staggered out.
They felt sick.
But they had to get to Boston.

The bear jumped onto a motorcycle.
The rhino climbed into a car
that was a little too small for him.
Dumbo told the man at the parking lot
that the circus would pay
for the cars and trucks.

Mrs. Jumbo rode in a big truck.
The tiger, the fox and the parrot
rode on top of her.
They had a very good driver.

Harry Hippo had his own little car. It went very fast.
The kangaroo found a wonderful new way to hop—
much faster than the old way!

At last the animals reached Boston.
Dumbo got them there just in time!

"Hooray," shouted the ringmaster.
"Let's get this circus started!"

"Boys and girls! The circus is about to begin,"
called the ringmaster. And begin it did.
Rhino and fox were swinging on their trapezes.
And so were the monkeys.

Mrs. Jumbo rolled around the ring on her ball.

Harry Hippo stood on his head.

Everybody was doing something.

It was truly the best circus anybody had ever seen.

When the circus was over, Mrs. Jumbo hugged Dumbo.
"Son," she said. "I am very proud of you.
Because of your help, the circus opened on time."

Then she added, "And you helped, too, Timothy."
Both Dumbo and Timothy were very, very happy.